P9-EJI-684

Tales of
Bunjitsu Bunny

Tales of
Bunjitsu Bunny

Written and illustrated by
John Himmelman

Henry Holt and Company
New York

WITHDRAWN

Henry Holt and Company, LLC
Publishers since 1866
175 Fifth Avenue
New York, New York 10010
mackids.com

Henry Holt® is a registered trademark of Henry Holt and Company, LLC.
Copyright © 2014 by John Himmelman
All rights reserved.
Library of Congress Cataloging-in-Publication Data
Himmelman, John, author, illustrator.
[Short stories. Selections]
Tales of Bunjitsu Bunny / written and illustrated by John Himmelman.—First edition.
    pages   cm
Summary: Although she can throw farther, kick higher, and hit harder than anyone else at
school, Isabel, aka Bunjitsu Bunny, never hurts another creature, unless she has to.
ISBN 978-0-8050-9970-6 (hardcover)
ISBN 978-0-8050-9972-0 (e-book)
[1. Martial arts—Fiction. 2. Rabbits—Fiction. 3. Animals—Fiction.] I. Title.
PZ7.H5686Taj 2014   [Fic]—dc23   2013048431

Henry Holt books may be purchased for business or promotional use. For information on bulk
purchases, please contact Macmillan Corporate and Premium Sales Department at
(800) 221-7945 x5442 or by e-mail at specialmarkets@macmillan.com.

First Edition—2014/Designed by Ashley Halsey
Printed in China by South China Printing Co. Ltd., Dongguan City, Guangdong Province

1 3 5 7 9 10 8 6 4 2

For my Hapkido and JKD family
at Green Hill Martial Arts

Contents

Introducing
Isabel

Isabel was the best bunjitsu artist in her school. She could kick higher than anyone. She could hit harder than anyone. She could throw her classmates farther than anyone.

Some were frightened of her. But Isabel never hurt another creature, unless she had to.

"Bunjitsu is not just about kicking, hitting, and throwing," she said. "It is about finding ways NOT to kick, hit, and throw."

They called her Bunjitsu Bunny.

The Locked Door

One afternoon, Isabel saw her fellow bunjitsu students outside their school. Teacher had left a sign on the door. It read, "Come on in."

"Teacher wants us to go inside," said Max. "But the door is locked."

"It is a test," said Kyle. "He wants us to kick the door open." Kyle kicked the door as hard as he could.

"OW!" he yelped, hopping up and down on one leg.

"No," said Betsy. "He wants us to punch it down with our fists!" They all punched the door with their mighty bunjitsu fists.

"Ow! OW! OOCH! OWEE OWEE OWEE!" they said. The door hadn't moved an inch.

"I have an idea," said Ben.
"What's the hardest part of our body?"

"The head," said Wendy.

"Right!" said Ben. "On the count of three, we will all perform the running bunjitsu head butt!"

"One . . . two . . ."

Suddenly, the door opened. Isabel was on the other side. "Come on in," she said. "Teacher is waiting."

"How did you get in?" asked
Betsy.

Isabel pointed to the open
window by the door and said,
"When the door is locked, go
through a window."

The Pirates

Isabel loved to take her rowboat out on the pond. The warm sun felt good as her boat rocked gently on the water.

Suddenly, another boat bumped into her. Four mean-looking foxes stared at her.

"We are pirates," said one of them. "Give us all your treasure!"

"I have no treasure," said Isabel.

"Then give us all your food!"

"I have no food," said Isabel.

"Then we will take you as our prisoner."

The pirates grabbed Isabel and
pulled her into their boat.

"If you have nothing to give us,
we will throw you in the water,"
said a pirate.

Isabel grabbed the arm of the nearest pirate and bunjitsu flipped him over her shoulder. He landed in her empty boat.

She then bunjitsu kicked the
second one so hard, he landed next
to his friend in her boat.

She threw the third pirate right on top of them.

The fourth pirate was so frightened, he crawled into her boat on his own.

"There," said Isabel. "Now you have my boat."

"We don't want your boat," said
a pirate. "It is too small for us."

"Can pirates swim?" asked Isabel.

"Of course!" they said.

"Good," said Isabel. "Because
your new boat is sinking."

Isabel sailed away. The warm sun felt good as her boat rocked gently on the water.

The Race

Sherman the tortoise loved to run, but he was always last in every race. No one wanted to race him because he was too easy to beat.

"I will race you to that tree across the field," said Isabel.

"You are Bunjitsu Bunny," said Sherman. "You will beat me very easily."

"Maybe, maybe not," said Isabel.

"On your mark. Get set. Go!"
Isabel shouted, and the race was on.
Isabel could have run right past
Sherman, but instead she stayed just
behind him.

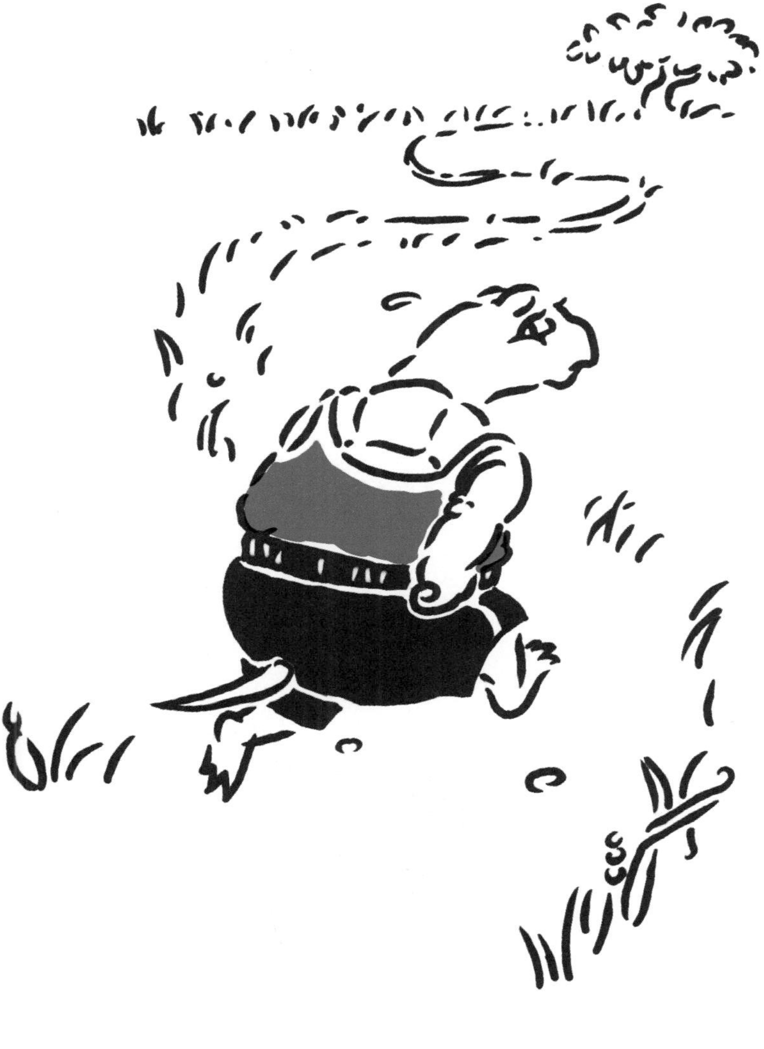

Sherman looked over his shoulder. *I am beating Bunjitsu Bunny,* he thought. He was so excited, he ran faster.

Isabel stayed right behind him. Whenever Sherman turned and looked, he saw she had almost caught him. This made him run even faster.

By the time he made it halfway to the tree, he was a blur of speed!

Sherman saw that Isabel was still right behind him. He gave it all he had. When he reached the tree, he was running so fast, he ran a whole extra mile before he could stop.

Finally, Isabel caught up.

"Did you let me win?" asked
Sherman.

"I did at first," she said. "But as
soon as you thought you could win,
you won."

The Challenge

"I challenge Bunjitsu Bunny to a fight," announced Jackrabbit. "I will be waiting for her at the marsh in three days. I will hit her so hard, she will fly to the moon!"

Isabel's friends told her about Jackrabbit's challenge.

"He is so big," said Kyle. "Are you afraid?"

"I am not afraid of big things," said Isabel.

"He is so fast," said Wendy. "Are you afraid?"

"I am not afraid of fast things," said Isabel.

"He is so strong," said Ben. "Are you afraid?"

"I am not afraid of strong things," said Isabel.

Three days passed. Jackrabbit
was at the marsh. Everyone waited
for Isabel.

They waited.

They waited.

And they waited some more.

Finally, they got tired of waiting and went home. Even Jackrabbit lost interest and hopped out of the marsh.

Max found Isabel in the sandbox at the playground.

"Here you are!" he said. "Why didn't you go to the marsh?"

"He said he was going to hit me," said Isabel.

"So you lost on purpose?"

"No, I did not lose," said Isabel. "He did not hit me."

Lucky Cricket

Cricket chirped sweetly in the garden.

"Is it true that crickets bring good luck?" asked Isabel.

"Very true," said Cricket.

"I have a big bunjitsu tournament next week. Will you stay with me for luck?"

"Yes," said Cricket. "First, I need to see how much luck you will need. Show me your bunjitsu moves."

Isabel knew a LOT of bunjitsu moves, so it took her many hours to show Cricket.

The next day, Cricket said to
Isabel, "Could you show me those
moves again?"

She showed him
all of her kicks,
blocks, strikes,
and flips—
EVERYTHING
she knew.

When Isabel finished, Cricket said, "I'm sorry. I dozed off. Could you show me again?"

Isabel was very tired, but she did as Cricket asked.

For the next few days, Cricket asked Isabel to show him all her moves. She showed him over and over and over again. *Cricket sure is forgetful,* thought the bunny.

On the day of the tournament,
Cricket joined Isabel.

She won contest

after contest

after contest!

At the end of the day, Isabel said,
"Thank you for bringing me luck,
Cricket!"

"You were the one who practiced
so hard every day," said Cricket. "I
just let you make your own good
luck."

Splash!

Isabel came upon her friends at the edge of a stream.

"Kyle kicked the ball across the water, and we need to get it back," said Betsy.

"I will get it," said Kyle.

First Kyle hopped onto a stump. Then he hopped onto the next stump. He tried to hop to the third stump. SPLASH! went Kyle into the water. He swam back.

"There's one way to get across this river," said Max. He grabbed a vine hanging from the trees. "EEEYYYAAAAA!" he shouted as he swung over the stream.

SPLASH! he went, as he fell in.

"I will try," said Betsy. She laid
a long stick across the stumps. She
balanced herself halfway across.

SPLASH! went Betsy into the
water. She swam back.

Isabel walked to the edge of the
stream and jumped in.

She climbed back out, grabbed
the vine, and swung over the water.

She dropped onto one of the
stumps. Hop, hop, hop she went,
across the stumps.

Then she walked across the stick
bridge to the other side.

Isabel picked up the ball and tiptoed over the stick bridge. A couple of hops and a swing later and she was back with her friends.

"Here is your ball," she said.

"You never needed to get wet,"
said Kyle.

"But once I did get wet," said
Isabel, "I didn't have to worry about
it anymore."

Butterfly

One day, Teacher said to his bunjitsu students, "I want you all to study an animal. In the next class, you will fight like that animal."

Isabel watched Butterfly in the meadow. "There are so many who want to eat you," she said. "And yet I see you in the meadow every day. Can you teach me what you do?"

"I would be honored to teach Bunjitsu Bunny," said Butterfly. "Try to catch me!"

Isabel tried to grab the slow-flying butterfly.

As soon as she got close, he quickly changed direction and flew away. She chased him all over the meadow. Whenever Isabel thought she had him, Butterfly surprised her with a burst of speed in a new direction.

The sun was going down, and it was time to go home.

"Thank you for teaching me," Isabel said to Butterfly.

The time came for the bunjitsu students to show what they learned.

Kyle studied a bear. He challenged Isabel.

Isabel strolled along the edge of the mats. Kyle charged straight at her. Isabel quickly changed direction. Kyle could not catch her.

Wendy studied a cat. She challenged Isabel. Isabel strolled along the edge of the mats. Wendy stalked her slowly . . . and pounced! Isabel quickly changed direction. Wendy could not catch her.

Betsy challenged Isabel. Betsy did not say which animal she studied. She and Isabel strolled along the edge of the mats.

Whenever Betsy got close, Isabel quickly changed direction.

Whenever Isabel got close, Betsy quickly changed direction. This went on and on and on.

Finally Teacher said to the class, "Everyone might as well have a seat."

"Who is winning?" asked Kyle.

"There will be no winner," said Teacher. "Now let's all sit and enjoy the two butterflies in the meadow."

Found

Isabel and her friends liked to play hide-and-seek. Isabel was very good at hiding. She could make herself disappear behind anything. And sometimes she could hide even when there was nothing to hide behind!

"Isabel probably makes herself invisible," said her friends.

"Isabel just flies away," said her friends.

"Isabel shrinks down to the size of a bug," said her friends.

One afternoon, Isabel found
a great place to hide. Her friends
looked and looked for her. They
looked for hours, but they could not
find her.

Soon it was suppertime. They
all went home. Isabel did not know
they had stopped looking for her.
She began to get lonely. She missed
her friends. She jumped down from
her hiding place and walked home
alone. *That was not so much fun,*
she thought.

The next day, Isabel and her friends played hide-and-seek again. Betsy closed her eyes and counted to ten while everyone hid. Isabel sat down behind her.

"Eight . . . nine . . . ten," said
Betsy. She turned around and saw
Isabel sitting on the ground.

"I found you!" said Betsy.

Isabel stood up and shook her hand. "Good job," she said.

"Why did you make it so easy?" asked Betsy.

"It is more fun to be found by friends than lost by friends," said Isabel. And she and Betsy ran off to find the rest of their friends.

The Nightmare

One night Isabel had a scary
dream. In her dream, she was chased
by monsters. She woke up very
frightened.

The next night, Isabel was afraid to go to sleep. She stayed up all night, practicing her bunjitsu to stay awake. She was very tired in school the next morning.

Later that night, Isabel kept every light on. She read books all night long. She knew if she fell asleep, the monsters would visit her.

When Isabel went to bunjitsu class the next day, Teacher asked, "Why do you seem so tired?"

"I can't sleep," said Isabel. "There are monsters in my dreams."

"Where do those dreams live?" asked Teacher.

Isabel pointed to her head. "In here," she said.

"Those monsters live inside the head of Bunjitsu Bunny?" he said. "I would be afraid to be THEM!"

Isabel smiled. Later that night, the monsters returned in her dream. This time they met with Bunjitsu Bunny. She sent those monsters away for good.

The Wave

"There is nothing more powerful than a wave," said Teacher. "If one can defeat an angry wave, one will be a true bunjitsu artist."

Isabel went to the beach. The
waves were crashing on the shore.

She walked up to a wave and
gave it her best kick.

The angry wave picked her up
and tossed her back on the beach.

Isabel stood firm and put out her
hands to block the next wave.

The angry wave picked her up
and tossed her back on the beach.

Isabel gathered all the power in her lungs and shouted in her loudest voice, "STOP!"

The angry wave picked her up
and tossed her back on the beach.

Isabel was tired of being tossed
around. She was about to give
the next wave a spinning bunjitsu
tornado fist, but she stopped.

Instead, she sat down and let the wave pick her up. She floated to the top and rode it gently down to the beach.

"This is so much more fun, Wave," she said. "Thank you!"

The wave gave her ride after ride until they both were tired.

The next day, Teacher asked, "Did you defeat the angry wave?"

"Yes," said Isabel. "It is no longer angry."

Bearjitsu Bear

Isabel was practicing her bunjitsu when Bear walked up to her.

"What are you doing?" he asked.

"It is called bunjitsu," said Isabel.

"Well, I practice *bearjitsu*," said
Bear. "It is much better than your
little bunny fighting."

"I am sure bearjitsu is good, too," said Isabel.

"What do you do in bunjitsu?" asked Bear.

"Well," said Isabel, "we kick pretty hard."

"Like this?" asked Bear. He kicked Isabel so hard she slid across the field.

"A little like that," said Isabel, dusting herself off.

"What else do you do?" asked Bear.

"We flip," said Isabel.

"Like this?" asked Bear. He grabbed Isabel's ears and flipped her to the ground.

"A little like that," said Isabel, straightening her ears.

"What else do you do?" asked Bear.

"We twist arms and legs," said Isabel.

"Like this?" asked Bear. He twisted Isabel into a pretzel.

"A little like that," said Isabel. "Please let go now."

"Do you give up?" asked Bear.

Isabel kicked Bear so hard he
shot straight into the clouds.

When he landed, she flipped him
to the ground so hard the earth
shook! Then she grabbed his giant
paw and twisted it behind his back.

"I give up!" shouted Bear.

"That's something I don't know how to do," said Isabel.

The Rock

One day, a big boulder rolled down the hill and landed in Isabel's yard.

"Oh no!" cried Isabel. "It crushed my flower garden." Isabel pushed and pushed the rock, but it would not move.

Then she found a large stick and rested it on a smaller rock. She pulled down as hard as she could to pry the big rock loose.

The stick broke. The rock did not move. Isabel's brother Max walked into the yard.

"Stand back!" he shouted. He ran
at the rock with a long stick.

The end of the stick struck the rock. He pole-vaulted so far over it that his sister lost sight of him.

"He'll find his way back in a few hours," said Isabel.

Isabel looked down and saw a little pink rock. She picked it up and placed it next to the boulder. It looked so pretty there. Then she placed another smooth white rock next to it.

Oh, how nice! she thought.

She placed a flat gray stone with the other rocks. Then she put a round one next to it.

Soon Isabel had covered the area
with stones of all colors and shapes.

Max found his way back and saw what she had done. "This looks great!" he said.

"One rock is just one rock," said Isabel. "Many rocks make a garden."

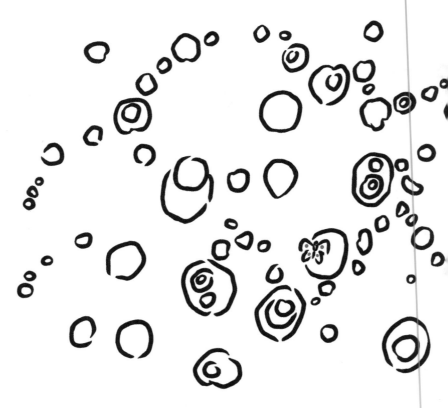

Later that night . . .

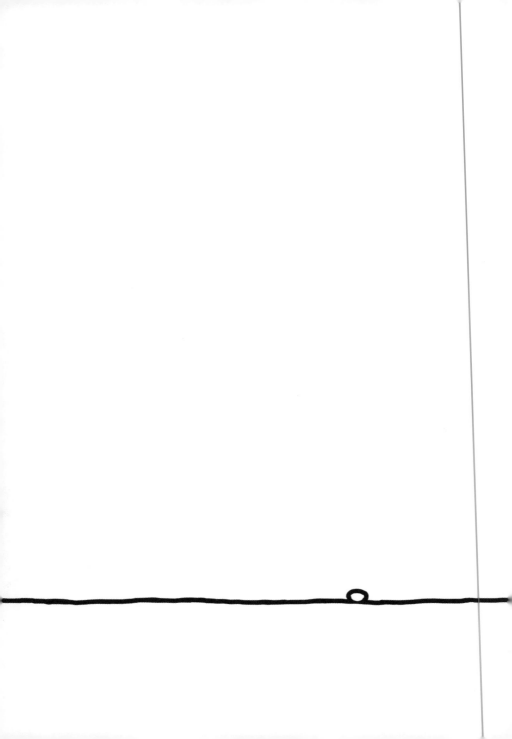

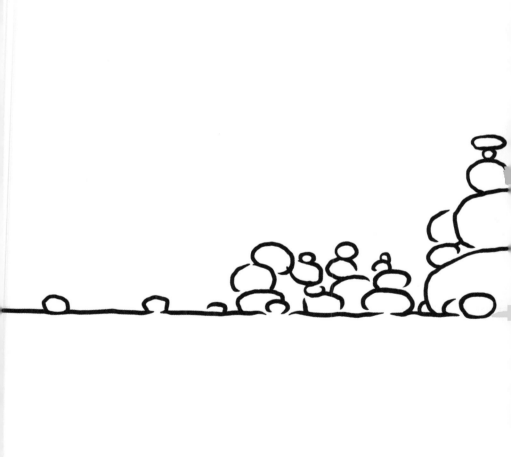

The Bunjitsu Code

All Bunjitsu students must do their best to follow the rules of Bunjitsu. If you wish to learn this art, you must read this and sign your name at the bottom.

I promise to:

- Practice my art until I am good at it. And then keep practicing.

- Never start a fight.

- Do all I can to avoid a fight.

- Help those who need me.

- Study the world.

- Learn from those who know more than I do.

- Share what I love.

- Find what makes me laugh, and laugh loudly. And often.

- Make someone smile every day.

- Keep my body strong and healthy.

- Try things that are hard for me to do.

Wendy   Betsy

Ben

MaX   KYLE

Isabel

31901056349592